PERIODIC COMPANIONS

for Thalia

PERIODIC COMPANIONS

Laynie Browne

friendship & admiration!

xoxo

Laynie

25 April 2018
nether Providence

**TINDERBOX
EDITIONS**

Tinderbox Editions
Molly Sutton Kiefer, Publisher and Editor
Red Wing, Minnesota
tinderboxeditions@gmail.com
www.tinderboxeditions.org

Cover design by Nikkita Cohoon
Cover art, "Untitled," by Noah Saterstrom, ink on paper 8" x 10".
  All drawings by Noah Saterstrom.
Interior design by Nikkita Cohoon
Author photo by Ryan Collerd

The images in this book are interpretations by Noah Saterstrom of the illustrations by Charles Louis Hinton in *Emmy Lou, Her Book and Heart*, by George Madden Martin, published by McClure, Phillips & Co., 1904.

Implicit is the hypothesis that all atoms of a given element behave in exactly the same way, irrespective of place and epoch.

—Rosmarie Waldrop

I could no longer ignore the fact that chemistry itself, or at least that which we were being administered, did not answer my questions.

—Primo Levi

with tender purloined sunlight
at winter's lip

—Lisa Jarnot

We are all semaphores for each other

—Inger Christensen

Born parenthetical subjects of a myopic regime, we strived to represent an unspoken sensibility, a nascent and covert counterculture—not the part of the culture that catered to us, but the part that ached, hungry for the dismantling of the complacencies that made daily life bearable but false.

—Pamela Lu

the tears are looking for a place to alight in, they aren't rain they're desolation
the tears are searching for you and will find you

—Alice Notley

Periodic Companions

To everyone in tears

Characters are based on the periodic table of elements:

C = Carbon

P = Phosphorus

Hg = Mercury

O = Oxygen

H = Hydrogen

As = Arsenic

Mg = Magnesium

Na = Sodium

Ag = Silver

S = Sulfur

Ne = Neon

Pt = Platinum

Li = Lithium

U = Uranium

P wondered about artists, academics, women and instability, considering that several of her oldest female friends had struggled with debilitating depression. She asks me what I think about the medicated life of HG for instance. I reply saying that I think it is his toxic institutional job that is destroying him. P tells me that *fragility* is what I should call it. Call what, I ask. But she does not answer. Maybe she is writing a talk or a paper about fragility. Maybe it is an important word to theorists like "disgust" or "failure." She might have been thinking out loud and not at all responding to what I asked her— which seems to be one symptom of this problem, or the inability to taste one's tea. It was really excellent tea, P said, and she had to have it every day at three or four o'clock but now she couldn't taste it any more.

This isn't fragility; it's desensitization. Is that why, writing a note to an old friend one rarely sees because of geography, when that friend has been diagnosed, it seems almost unfeeling to write something about her radiance? Does it come off as wooden because that isn't the way we speak? But P isn't listening, she's been desensitized and gets up abruptly and leaves without saying goodbye. She's that volatile. She swirls her white coat over her shoulders and is gone, liberated as a vapour. See what I mean about the way that we speak or do not speak? Well chosen words act like a clasp. But the reason P gets up and bristles is that it is too close to her own scrape, a sidelong conversation we've never had but clearly both intimate. Is it because she is here that we don't have the conversation? Does muddled geography make some admissions simpler? Who is the one beside you, and who is the one you rarely manage to meet but understands you best? That is the kind of question HG would ask: Who is that *you*, when you are at your computer screen? This is fragility, instability. How much easier it is when we are all at our computer screens. And how bleak.

P's point, however, is not lost upon me, though she made it by saying nothing. She thinks that in order to create a fiction I must remove myself farther from any memory of non-fiction. But then I remind her that she herself is not even a fabrication drawn from various real-life companions. She is completely fictional. Still, I have no control over her actions and she does not listen because she does not believe me. P argues that appearance, properties and structures can change at any moment. She strikingly often does not resemble herself. For many years I did not remember her and she could not recognize herself as she passed between various bodies, depending upon her surroundings and partners. If she can resemble graphite, if she can be found in pesticides, toothpaste and detergents, where is she located exactly?

I first met P when we were still young enough not to know how little we knew. She was sitting in a corner of a very dark café, at a waxy colorless table. We had several friends in common, so I walked over and sat down. I thought she was highly reactive, based on what I'd heard, but then I didn't know that she was never a free floating element. She was reading. I looked down at the text discussing explosives, nerve agents, friction matches. She looked up and did not exactly express pleasure at seeing me, but she did eventually emit a faint glow. Even if she felt green, even if she had been stoppered in a jar, which at times she seemed to have nearly been, she still could emit some visible light. I can't explain exactly what happened next, maybe because her reaction time is slow, by which I mean she didn't begin to emit the light right away, but the more time we spent together the more I was sure that I never saw flame nor felt any heat, and yet I thought of her as a bearer of something essential in my makeup, not a cold chemical reaction but more like I had evaporated, or she had become a conductor of electricity, puckered sheets, linked several states of myself. As if she were already in my bones quietly waiting to be discovered.

Though P was rarely quiet and I was later to learn all about her reactive qualities. Once P told me that the reason she never felt this way before (*this way*, meaning the desire for a particular state of being we had yet to create language to articulate) was that she did not have the right persons to feel this way with. You might wish to be enamored, she argues, if you believe it possible for yourself or anyone, but that doesn't mean that you can just enlist whoever is beside you. This seems an unlikely observation considering that P has fallen in love so many times—perhaps as often as I have written the alphabet.

No, she demands, dismissing my suggestion. But love was a type of shorthand for which we have never found a better or less objectionable word. We therefore agreed that we were talking about unification or the opposite of fragility and instability and also about the ability to emit light and all practices that could possibly point one in that direction. O once said that he was interested mostly in ecstatic practices and that's why he chose drugs. P wondered why he didn't mean sex. HG says that he has no need for love and H says that everything she has ever done has been motivated by romantic desire. AS is shocked anyone could entertain such ideas. P says her notion has nothing to do with love but it does have to do with desire—not for a person or anything physical, but desire to act within a landscape, as catalysts for others taking action. P says it could be about anything relevant: hunger, or shorebirds, or it could be electric cars, or education, but she wants to effect change on a level that is difficult to describe—molecular or cellular— or to change our memory as a species. This is why HG is in love with something like systems theory. O, who is agnostic, claims there is no relationship between these concepts, and H always disagrees.

There was no name for P's book. She said this was because she had not written it yet. It did not exist. Often, because it was difficult to write the book, as many times as she had fallen in love, or I had written the alphabet, she decided to do something simpler, like searching for chestnut flavored green tea. Once while we were browsing in a warehouse sized international import market she asked me, what made anything hers to tell? I had no answer for her, since she didn't want to tell anything. But what did that matter, she continued after a moment. And she went on to claim that writing is not about belonging, it's more about thievery. When she said *not belonging* what she meant was that language doesn't belong to anyone in particular, so her statement about thievery is only as serious as the notion that one could steal what cannot be owned. When we returned she wrote the words, *untellable, unsayable,* and *indivisible* as potential titles. Then she crossed them all out and went to boil some water. The next page in her journal was blank. It appeared a lovely crème color and one could see both vertical and horizontal striations in the paper. It looked perfect with nothing written on it. When I remarked on this she picked up the book and turned her back to me. I hadn't meant it as a discouragement. I hadn't meant anything at all beyond the pleasing sight of paper and blankness. Blankness as an invitation. Paper a welcome covering.

It looked perfect with nothing written on it. And other things one should not say to one's reactive friends. But still, part of the problem was that there was no shorthand for what P wanted to say, and what she wanted to say, even though she would adamantly oppose the idea of saying anything, was that she had not yet lived what she wanted to write. This was a paradoxical aspiration however, because we did not believe in autobiography, or memoir, or storytelling, or non-fiction, or narrative as ways to approach writing. We knew that we were both potentially fictional, or we hoped to become so in order to experience the complete liberty of two-dimensional characters. This was not cynical on our part because we believed the ability to invent ourselves completely necessary in order to invent anything else. Our notions were hypothetical, as we had not figured out an escape from the obvious difficulties of being three-dimensional persons in a non-fictional world. We knew we needed to know something and to dictate nothing. We had no interest in recounting, retelling, or writing about something that had already occurred.

If the writing itself is the event then why can't I figure it out by writing, P asked. You can, I answered, knowing that we hadn't yet, and I thought, while you write— time passes and you discover things and then you try hard not to be didactic or to think too hard about ideas of artifice or confession and you realize the difficulty of your task. We still live within pages and persons and within our own limited consciousness.

P argues that if we can experience this shorthand for love, for which we have no name and by which we really mean something else entirely (HG says it is a metaphor for love) then we can write something as if we (meaning she) did not write it. And that is my goal, she says. To write something not written by me. If I could do that it would be the same thing as this shorthand. She is frustrated with our lack of a name for this shorthand for something indescribable and decides that we must give it a name. She pulls out a dictionary opens it at random and points her finger to a word. Then she asks me to name the word.

She looks at me oddly because I am not saying anything and the reason is that she has placed her index finger on a place on the page where there is no writing whatsoever. Of course, we and our companions can generally be located in the margins, so we shouldn't be surprised. I tell her, you've touched the white space. This is impossible, she says, angrily, handing me the book.

I look at the book and tell her that the first word on the page she has picked is "garnet" and the last word on this same page is "garret." She looks up, mildly interested. And then she emits something. She is quiet for a moment, percolating. Then finally she says, that works. I will refer to our "it" as either, garnet, or garret— *depending*.

"Depending?" I ask. We hinge upon how anything is going at a given moment. We are either garnet or garret. And who would think that the change of just one little letter, an "r" or an "n" could make such a difference?

At that time P had met AS but she did not really know him except through stories she had heard about him, all of which seemed to sway a particular gravity for her but which remained for me entirely unreliable analogues. Of his friends he said little, but he was bound in various secret and interlocking societies. He traveled to France, Germany, Italy and Romania.

So what— I said, about his travels, his ellipsoidal formation of men. So what— to his ill-defined though apparently profitable chemical compound business. P recognized something in him which I can only now begin to understand. In the same way that she did not resemble herself, AS also had the talent to be something other. But while P maintained the ability to look different from herself, AS seemed to morph in more dramatic ways. She called him her darling allotrope.

So what— I said, but she continued to ignore me, to write about failure, about women and fragility, and to read about volcanic ash, roxarsone and mineral ores.

The symptoms of AS thrashing were manifest in many ways. I had watched others fail at his glance. As a protective measure I began to collect evidence. His tone was metallic. What was he made of? His gravity changed at will. And then his tone was not metallic. His complexion appeared to tarnish in certain weather and when conversation grew heated. His eyes were steel grey and his expressions brittle. His friends called him *Paris Green* and *Poison of Kings*. When angry, he fumed. And worse, though it sounds antiquated and entirely inappropriate, women in his presence are prone to eat vinegar and chalk, to talk of how to improve their complexions. They appear pale. They quit their jobs. He claims that their suffering is purely accidental, and then goes off to attend to various alchemical concerns, such as the purity of drinking water.

When I first knew P she was narrow, thin, transparent, and nervous. She was the most amative person I had ever met. She was greatly susceptible to others' impressions, to light, to sound, to smell, and to electrical changes. She once fainted during a thunderstorm. She was sudden in everything and had violent reactions. These qualities could at times irritate and even inflame me but strangely we did not degenerate. Her fits bound us further.

After she met AS, she liked the dark, to lie on her right side, to eat cold food, to be in the open air, and washing with cold water. She took to her bed for long spells. She hated to be touched, loathed physical or mental exertion, twilight, warm food or drink, changes of weather, lying on her left side, and ascending stairs. This was difficult because AS lived at the top of a four-story walk-up.

But this is not where this garnet or garret begins. It begins with my visitation to a place where I went in search of garnet or garret. I feared, at that particular moment in time, the diagnosis of MG, and that this moment of waiting, while I had no bad news to contemplate, might be a last moment of innocent happiness. MG's illness had lodged itself in my body. I was not sure how I would explain this to the person I was about to meet, NA, a woman I had been told had a gift for the art of correspondences.

The building was being gutted, or so it appeared, as the ceiling unveiled revealed hanging wires and fixtures of all kinds, metal appliances, walls seen in several dimensions in their true sedimentary nature. I was uncertain about how to open the door to the building. Does one ring? No, I was told by some persons with the familiarity of assuming residents. Up the steps and round the corner I went, certain I had entered the inside of my own untethered interior, as if someone had made a cinematic sketch of my skull.

I sat beside NA, who began asking me questions in a looping manner in order to prescribe a remedy with an orderly like equals like trace of a substance she termed rare. What is it, I asked expectantly. But she did not give me any answer, saying that before she could make a diagnosis she would need to read my writing. This was the beginning of many conversations I would have with NA, while I gazed at a delicate mobile and various art assemblages upon the walls of her office.

The garret begins like any illness, like my concern, along with P's, about artists, academics, women and instability. My garret continued to grow along with the results of several of MG's scans, and with P's growing association with AS. Before the diagnosis of MG I walked into rooms with bright white halls and plenty of light. When I was hungry I ate and when I was tired I slept. All of these things gave me pleasure, even the pleasure of frustration when *place* or *haunt* or relationships went awry. I firmly believed in the immortality of every-one I loved. When the diagnosis kept repeating itself until MG had undergone what seemed endless tortures I found that the rooms with bright white halls and the shoes on my feet and the clothes on my back seemed useless things. It was not that I was ungrateful, but rather that suddenly the pale of my days, or the pall of my days, or perhaps there is not any way to tell what kind of days they were— suddenly became thick and vapid, possibly prehistoric. It seemed ironic that P and I were so adamant in our notions that art had nothing to do with telling and that the commonest of experiences such as sickness and loss could prove to be so isolating. Part of the problem was the invisibility of the situation. The *invisibles* were more difficult to treat simply because they had reached this state of the unsayable that we had hoped to achieve in art. I was disgusted but also believed that the profundity of my misery would permanently mark me, and that this was what we wanted, to be marked and scarred. We wanted our faces to be lined and our hands to hold the impressions of everything we touched. So the place or the garnet or the garret changed hands or changed mouths once more and I thought of my unutterable place as "the scathes" as if that were a location, as if the conventions of language were of any consequence. We did not want to live a life unscathed. It was impossible, in any case, and anything we might attempt to potentially help others could certainly not come from an unmarked existence.

We were all part of these invisibles, as persons having maladies not describable or necessarily treatable by any recognized methods. I talked at length with NA about these questions, even about the scathes and our various unnamable plights. She was the only medical artist I'd ever met. She spun past me various remedies and though she was very empathetic she did not have any suggestion for how to counter the invisibles, except to write.

NA was blond and bright-faced though soft and unimposing. Her concern seemed to cascade down the curve of her face. She was a solid outline, abundantly present. She sat in her straight backed chair upon wheels and occasionally peered at her computer screen and typed something or clicked as we talked. She loaned me books. She was a good listener and there was something so pleasing about the process of talking and then taking home not a plan or a frightening and expensive pharmaceutical, but a vial of tiny round white pills that dissolved under the tongue and had absolutely no physical repercussions. And the name of the material from which the pills were made was always replete with suggestion; for instance, she had given me something made from diamond, and later something from salt. She had given H something made from a tiny plant whose name I cannot recall. But she said that it grew at high elevations, was solitary, and associated with dreaming. We had, all of us, at one time or another, been to see her, especially in the dark of the year.

We all wondered, does it really exist, the space between us and also what binds us when we no longer inhabit our bodies? In this way I was being called to assist P in articulating something we had yet to know. MG's diagnosis prepared me. We had not chosen these events and we were acutely aware of this fact, as well as the sunny illusion that seems to follow when we are flooded with desirable events. It is easy to believe we deserve a flood of good fortune. But when the flood is hideous, when the body fails, we have the strong wish that we are dreaming. I was aware when packing of a need to pick garments that afforded protection. Then I looked out the window of the plane longingly at the city I was leaving. When I arrived I learned that MG had difficulty balancing. Medications had affected the nerves in the bottoms of her feet. I gave her a bell so that so she could know I was nearby, but also be free of me completely.

When I returned to our scathes my attention continued to turn in multiple directions—out towards MG and the possible redemptive quality of tears, and inward toward person or page, to include the smudge of personhood which made anything plausible. In a time of toxic arrangements and irritations it would make most sense to conclude that we no longer knew how to embody love or necessary alphabets. We no longer carry our letters, our signatures of meaning, hands curled around instruments. Instead we scroll and voice and strain our eyes over pulsing screens. We rarely look up and our hands, moving madly, no longer know how to curl. On the train young women sit together but do not look up at each other, engrossed as they are in their hand-held attachments. What is signified when proximity to breathing bodies is disregarded in favor of attachments?

During a winter storm many of us were stranded together in a garret of our own making. We sat at a sloping table HG had made from several planks found in a dumpster and hurriedly painted in shiny hues of silver and white. He looked down clasping his teacup. P and AS were in one corner, ignoring the rest of us. O was agitated in the somewhat stifled atmosphere of the room. We watched the snow in livid streaks and heard the traffic below. H however had a plan for our movement to a livelier space. She had a new acquaintance, AG, she wanted us to meet. AG was hosting a gathering and did we want to come? P and AS eyed the pile of coats in the corner and slumped back down saying nothing. Nobody moved. Then H got up to go and I joined her. Within moments we had left the garret and were trudging toward an unknown assemblage.

It was the last days of what O called azure light. We fell back. Trudging through winter had nothing to do with punctuation or spelling a thing before us. Not knowing was a passport. I worried that H's idea of a gathering might involve characters sorting tables, places to sit, colors to wear in photographs, all of which P and I found abhorrent. Persons hyperventilating at the charge bill. Or not. It was not that H was superficial but that she moved fluidly in any social situation. She possessed the mysterious ability to admire anyone. After a while I turned to look behind to see that HG and P and AS were following us not far back, walking in similar strides in the tracks we had already pressed into the snow.

And so we entered into a chapter which P later described in her book as escorting what only the invisible may escort. Despite her valiant captioning efforts I am loyal to every moment as I imagine it, to my own personal "scathes" as well as to our collective. The building was a brownstone, with a winding staircase three floors up. We knocked at the door and heard jeering and shuffling behind. No one came so we entered. Several clusters of persons stood. Candles and blue glass lanterns illuminated the space. Here I must arrest my sloppy exuberance. Illusion will be metered and held against my lack. Here is the place I may write to the blankness and emptiness in which I imagine AG. Our initial conversation, when I attempt to break into language, finds me always in tears. The confusion must not be all my own. How frightening to not resist the real subject, beyond person. How easy to see a human face in this guise—as a gate. How easy to contemplate skin and fail. How simple to fall, lean, look down, awaken. How ripping to continue remembering from where we have come, for what reason. I wish to return to the place where daily habit does not interfere with the intermediary gravity of bodies fallen together as one.

We plummeted into what appeared to be a painted nocturnal scene when I supposed we had been walking in daylight. And then we were lost counting flat grey unmarked passages. H led me to a place she called her garret or garnet, which she simply referred to as "G." I appropriate that shorthand at times, already twice removed, though O and HG and P were all adamantly opposed to her use of "G." So I began to say 'Place' instead, or better yet *place*, because for me it was still just a placeholder for something I could not name and had not yet experienced.

I went with H reluctantly one night. High white walls were covered with rugs and on wooden benches sat many people with eyes closed. Musicians were singing in a language I did not recognize and I thought this is not the *place*. But I didn't scoff like HG or O or even P would have, nor did I immediately join as H did, linking arms with strangers. All around was erratic movement and I was suddenly ill —muffled, twisted. Everything appeared as though through a distant tunnel. At first I was a watcher and then the tunnel turned or blemished. Was I a person in a room, in a *place*, which had not been determined as previously existing? AG was saying something upon which faces turned, cascaded. My cheeks were wet. Rivulets, tunnels pulled. I was bothered by the way my face contorted. What had become of volition? In a doorway questions hovered whispering. The ill hallway plummeted again, bled a path saying go—.

All persons seemed not to have occurred. What was our medium? Non-thoughts pulled taut. Whose face interrupted, gone? AG's words hung in the air in several dimensions. We saw identity through a false glass. We began removing panes. Eventually I found that I loved the far corner of a sofa. By late in the evening I was waiting at the window for release.

P calls this emotional ventriloquism but H says that it means I have located a desire I had previously kept secret from myself. O, who hates the word "longing," would later proclaim that I must have been fighting something off. HG agreed, adding that I had been looking exhausted. In that moment, however, I was far from our collective thoughts— muffled sideways seeing continued. What is the purpose of distraction? The music was nonverbal, sound and gesture reaching a pitch. Movement was color. People were loudly embracing, without any self-consciousness, all types, as you would only find in such a submerged urban lair: dreadlocks, willowing, blue hair, piercings, wide awake among mobs of children, gauzy see-through fabrics, stacked heels and bare feet, essential oils and a scent-free seating section. Sideways anticipation synapse has us setting out to untoward places. Who will we be later? An occasional suit, bling and young collegiate professionals there only to meet a potential date. What do we fear— within the song and a certain intention, as H would later say, though I had no idea what she meant. Many foldings and convolutions passed before I was able to investigate the initial, untaught seeds of night.

What I knew in that moment was that I had been missing. There was a place, my placeholder, unacknowledged until this moment. It reared up awkwardly and I stifled it as well as I could. A place, I later had to admit, internally located and overlooked, at once empty, remote, and unpracticed, which begged the shorthand for love of which we often spoke, but could not write, which was related to other creative or political acts but not the same. This was the opposite of trying to write and also identical with the impulse to write a book one hadn't written oneself. It had more to do with standing pressed within a crowd, with being indistinguishable, than it did with being recognizable. P calls it receiving but not projecting. So the impulse to cry had been merely my first unwilling recognition of this nameless place. P would not cry; instead she would turn to vapor and vanish into another. O would endlessly categorize, pontificate and quote philosophy. HG turned to drama or was ironic and dismissing. H simply merged with whoever was nearest. I hadn't found any place or practice and yet I had found another placeholder and it had nothing to do with an individual self as I understood the concept at the time. I later thought of this as a non-physical place, a state of being, a way to practice whatever it was we were trying so desperately to name, possibly, who to be.

I internalized a way of thinking and talking about what this meant, a type of reframing of reality through contemplative practices which I glimpsed first from H and then from AG and S. Later I witnessed a woman in a crowd sobbing. Her face was lifted — open—tears ran down her face. She did not obscure her features. This modest display soon became a goal which I have yet to achieve: to cry openly and unapologetically in public. I had no inkling at the moment of the import tears would later have for us. I began to wonder about contortion, shame, the suppression of emotion and how this might relate to artists, academics and instability. I began to wonder about how certain practices or ways of living might replace, supplement or improve upon what we know about medication and various traditional forms of healing. I began to wonder about this question of public space, communal activity and shame. I began to wonder if a public artistic space could exist outside certain expectations of academic, institutional, or patron based standards. I had had glimpses of such spaces and they tended to have other rules— philosophy we read and often misinterpreted. Parroted, not lived.

I had spent my whole life being taught that material accumulation was the key to success and that success was the only viable alternative for a woman aspiring to any identity other than that of "wife." I had now begun the onerous task of unlearning everything that had come before. In order to internalize this new way of thinking I needed to surround myself with persons who wanted similarly to undo various notions of the world. P was the first. She taught me to cook foods I'd never even seen (as a well-endowed "wife" or a successful woman wouldn't need to cook at all), to dance (as another language) and to sit on a windy bench overlooking the ocean with a notebook in hand. Or I should say she was my accomplice in these practices. She taught me to get arrested in peaceful protests. She changed her hair color and her boyfriends at an alarming rate. At that time I also learned to sit at a place on the coast where the ocean spit violently in time with my unruly thoughts. P was the only one I would occasionally take with me. She could convulse voluminously saying nothing and she tolerated my earliest attempts to write.

Many years later, when P was diagnosed I imagined us sitting on the same bench, and at the same spot on the coast, and I could not reconcile the sound of her medicated voice, her uncertainty. She who had always been so certain. Her instability, her fragility, and her book— she couldn't write about it because it had not happened yet. Still she was asking herself the same questions about women and dissolution. Paradox— what has not happened yet is more interesting than the past, which is fixed. In the eventual present is a place to reside. This is not the same as the future. It is the place easiest to overlook because its unfixed aliveness makes us uncomfortable. Requiring presence by virtue of turning to meet a particular face is what I'll call our project. It belongs to everyone though it is not quite transcribable. This is one of the inherent problems in trying to meet the paradoxical face. To write it, in most instances, is to step out of the stream. Except when it isn't. You may also meet another foil, an overused screen. I am careful to try to avoid the blankness which comes from not living. Nothing is chronological. When quiet surrounds me as a hedge I am grateful.

But then again quiet is also a culprit. O says that inaction is the price of contentment. P reminds me that transformation occurs when we are not content. But I cannot remind her of this now, meds out of sync, between jobs, lovers, uncertain. It was much easier to view such uncertainty as a necessary balm when we were barely twenty years old, at that spot on the coast, nothing yet inscribed.

I asked P to tell me where she had been with AS. This is what she wrote.

thi s is wh a tw as

And then she fell asleep.

Later, much later, she talked. The last days of the year spun letters into new formations, typed insistence on who we weren't. The spindle was terrible— in such perfection— of what was drowning a face— as if one life drawn in resemblance of another held what you might call insistence.

She was drowning by face and by night and not by candlelight so you might say.

Dredging aside, she flew through his fingers and returned as silt. They had come, obviously, not to abstain, but to partake in a crammed false sort of light. They discussed parties as a type of torture. P laughed not because she did not agree but because his reasons were so elegantly articulated and because he refused to ever behave elegantly with her alone. Only in company could he appear with such lovely manners. His objection was to continual interruption.

Interruption?

Yes, you begin a conversation, and then someone cuts in.

She saw very well how this could be true and added that what she found particularly gruesome was the endless driving—then entering each gathering and becoming oriented to its particular dramas. She said this as they sat in traffic on remote freeways where one might change from the XE to the RA and if one appears late the hostess may break into tears, so that each day of one's vacation one must rise early and prepare for the day's events and personages.

It's the personages, he said, which make you tired.

Clearly, she added. And what is even worse is trying not to be ill.

From indulgences? That isn't what bothers you most.

I'd rather be alone in a cave. Either there is terrible friction or one is completely bored.

You have to go to the *outskirts*—we must.

The dining is better.

She pictures a skirt and how to walk out—upon its edges. Though clearly, she would rather gather in the dead center, find herself brightly affixed.

We'd be brilliant, he adds, to escape them all.

I would not be myself without the city. The city perplexed.

I did not long for material things or even the lives of others but for the idea of a life that was not purely singular—to live vicariously and enmeshed, sleeping tangled in a puzzle of perspectives. What I wanted was not to be only myself, meaning I wanted to see from vantages not limited by my own. There is nothing singular in this desire except that I was often surrounded by people who wished the opposite. Narcissistic or solipsistic, I wanted none of it—which was why certain periodic companions were irreplaceable. All of us flawed in our insistence in one way or another, myself in what P called *my habits of outskirts*, and she idealizing a type of intimacy that works best in theory.

At AG's gatherings P was tentative. Often, it was me, H and HG. O was against these gatherings but always wanted to know everything that happened. I wasn't sure if this was because he was secretly curious or if he only wanted to be able to dismiss our jaunts. O did not trust AG, and because he had never met AG, you could say that he did not trust the idea of AG. This seemed ridiculous to me but still we obliged O by recounting.

Don't call it a scene, said H.

What then, we asked.

"G," she would say.

"Place," I would echo. But then O came up with a recalibration of our earlier *garnet* or *garret,* calling our visits the *garish haunts*. This sounded almost goth and that couldn't have been further from where we were. After a while I stuck with just *haunts*. There wasn't any single meeting place but often we were at AG's loft and the set up was usually the same: cushions on the floor and a dilapidated samovar filled with strong tea, milling about, sitting in silence, and finally we would listen to someone talk or perform. At first we remained in the back, not knowing anyone, with no entrée into the deeper recesses of the place.

I developed a series of questions I wanted to ask but noted that questions were usually ignored. Often there were unanswerable questions regarding political violence. Some asked questions which were too personal to be addressed in company. Many just wanted to hear themselves talk and did not articulate questions. After a time I noticed that something had changed in relation to the *haunts*. I began to depend on these excursions mostly for the periods of silence.

Some of my questions dissolved, others emerged and I could hear them revolving in various formations but they did not urgently press. Rather, they were the kind of questions with which one must co-exist. I didn't expect AG or anyone else to answer them. I didn't understand how the silence had changed me. H had similar experiences which we couldn't discuss using language. Without speech we sympathized with each other's non-material thoughts. If I tried to describe them here I would certainly fail and in this failure is a kinship with the failed project of trying to articulate a placeholder for what we could not name. Instead of struggling with this inability I inclined warmly toward our earlier losses, the days spent gazing at a blank page, walking streets in aimless unison, tiny words scrawled to stand in for all that we did not say.

We met S at one of AG's gatherings. HG noticed him leaning on the mantle over the fake fireplace filled with candle lanterns. His eyes appeared almost yellow and his hands were shaking. He was talking to AG in a very animated manner. Later we learned that they had been arguing about something said by NE, whom we didn't know. Amid the clamor we heard the phrases "screaming at statues," "backwards inscriptions," "repetition and isolation," and "deconstructing social norms." How to interact or how to co-exist was something we talked about a lot, mostly noting that no one could dictate such things, but still we kept trying. For instance we did not approve of or I should say we did not buy the notion of success as credentialed. AG once said that there were two ways to become anything. One was to go to school and obtain a particular document. The other way, he muttered, was jagged. The point he was trying to make was not that one shouldn't go to school but that doing so didn't necessarily mean that you were what the paper said. The way to be a writer, obviously, was to write. The way to learn something about shorthand, garret, haunt, and questions of how to live was obviously to be alive. It was already happening but we wanted to know how to speed up our understanding. We wanted to know how to talk and write about questions of personhood and our planet and politics—without doing it horribly. Most difficult was to talk about the invisible without immediately being turned out from any gathering. We could talk and write about cultural inheritance. We could joke about our religious or non-religious upbringings. We could talk about meditation and maybe even "practice" but if we went any further we were shunned, even among each other. That's why we couldn't say "G" for garret or garnet. We all had experiences which made us consider the statement "we have decided not to die." There was of course no language for these experiences but we remembered them together and we knew that "identity is a disease" was the closest thing we could imagine to both inhabiting a body and also boundlessness.

S, as it turned out, ignored the taboo and the phobias of the intellectually bent and talked about everything as if he simply knew. But he was also humble, and possibly manic. This seemed, ironically, to have a stabilizing effect on HG, who stopped teasing P about AS and stopped mocking H's attempts to get us all to various gatherings. He even listened patiently while she explained the benefits of inversions. A new epoch began for HG, who, within days of this fateful meeting could be seen walking arm in arm with S and saying nothing cynical.

HG was trying to guess the age of AG. He thought that he was very old.

What do you mean by very old, asked O. Do you mean ancient?

He couldn't be, said H.

Why not, said HG. I think he must be at least biblical.

Very funny, said O. He does live in a slag dump.

Please, stop, said S.

He is very ductile and malleable, added HG.

P then irritably interjected that AG was the most stable and pure person she had ever met.

At this AS lifted an eyebrow and remarked that it was always a cloudy day on the days that we met him.

It's winter, remarked HG.

He isn't pure, said AS. I've seen him tarnish.

This was all too much for H, who concurred with P, called him brilliant and highly electrical. H's statement bothered HG and O, who began to argue about low contact resistance and luster, and suggested we attempt a form of carbon dating to determine his age. S intervened by throwing his arm about HG. H, who we all secretly thought might be involved with AG, retreated to a corner with one of AG's books in her hand and a drowned look, but she said nothing. We did not question her because there was no one she did not love.

I didn't think that AG's age was very important but I did note that he seemed to be the best reflector of visible light and that he took wonderful photographs. He was a rare and expensive superconductor. But I did not say this aloud. I also noted but did not remark that since P had met him she seemed less phobic. When I first knew her she suffered from stage fright, claustrophobia and anxiety in the face of unexpected situations. But now she was less likely to suggest that something awful was about to happen, for example, being crushed in a dissolving building.

HG said it was as if he were waiting in an aquarium, only with no water. In the Institute his co-workers talked in lines, in rivets, always with something in hand. He referred to them as "insiders." He'd say, "I'd rather be blizzarded, fraught, why should I?" And they replied with something like publicity. He explained to us that "insiders" see everything as how to get a certain number. A number being a goal, a determinant, a presentiment. That's what you get, they say, further, further. A number—being a number of bodies or a number of promises. A number which replenishes an ever dwindling coffer of doubt. "Insiders" wanted coverage, a time-piece studded with workers who didn't own their own work, or the language they used, or their time, or what they were required to wear or consume. "You know" they said, as if anything regarding this arrangement might change, but they didn't see change as possible within the weight of their consigned bodies. They presented HG with deadlines and rubrics and committees and three-year plans, all in the name of—. No one remembered *the name.* They made more work for themselves by hiring others to create language that they then rewrote until it was all uniformly in the voice of *the name.* They did not know exactly why they did this except that it was expected. There was something to maintain, a consistency. They announced things at podiums—not looking but grasping the edges of the always high tech podiums—as if it might be merely finely wrought metals which supported them.

The 'other possibles' as he called them didn't hold to the same rigorous procedures as "the insiders" but they presented alternately baffling predicaments, such as to suggest to him who he should be. He was not diminished except in proclamations such as *what exactly did you mean?* And also, the 'other possibles' didn't know things and didn't want to know them, things that HG and the rest of us knew. But when he suggested anything they said, almost diminishing his breath, that they didn't want to know. So they didn't. For instance he suggested that they bring PT, who was brilliant and beloved. But they had not heard of PT and then in almost the same breath they claimed they did not like PT. We knew it was a no-brainer to bring PT and that the 'other possibles' were simply not knowing what they didn't want to know, which we all found sad. They did not know the names of the most beloved artists of our generation, and neither did the podium graspers know many of these names that we knew from having read and from wanting to know, and from sleeping on couches in various cities and taking buses or trains or road trips. The podium graspers claimed to have already brought everyone of any note whatsoever (meaning numbers, repetition of what they knew, promises) but they had not. And the 'other possibles' who didn't want to know what we knew felt neglected and safe in what they did actually know. This left us, of course, with the implausible task of unlearning the "insiders" and informing the 'other possibles' of what they did not wish to learn. We realized that we must forge a new way.

What a relief it was when we all entered the quagmire of AG's ongoing and unplanned salon to find writers wrestling on the ground in tights and wolf head masks, half naked, living in dilapidated ruins, their children playing with string, placing penguins in cars which drove of their own volition, having read all the maps of the world, and therefore always knowing where a penguin needed to go. In other words, their children knew the future. They knew that lions spoke in lion English and lion French, and would create paintings of their speech in brown and orange on paper. The wrestling threadbare paint smeared poets were not about numbers of bodies or numbers of accounts. When they needed resources they would offer a charade or read your cards between conference panels over tea and then use these insights to imagine how things might unfold. Above all they were fond of each other in a way that magnetized various situations as visibly as capes and frocks and glitter. They mostly did not own places to live or plans of numbers but they did own what they thought and how they lived on top of each other in boxes and cutouts. They did not begin or end on time but they were never bored in the work which was theirs collectively, not as a number or as a presentiment but as a way to pull bodies together in time. The promise was to show up, not as an attempt to attract the 'other possibles' or the "insiders" or anyone who wasn't of the tribe. To be of the tribe meant that you were here, in the wrestling lateness. We had a non-place—or the garret or haunt became wherever we spoke, created images, dramatized, filmed, named, or somatically explored. We did not have a place for the happenings, which occurred between persons. We did not separate our bodies or our thoughts from the happenings. When we saw this for the first time it was like we had all left the empty aquarium and entered the wild though obliging ocean. It was like coming home inside someone else's body, if one body could be many, like the one time when P and I had walked along the beach and it began to rain and then it was as if we had swum. The ocean was in our ears and our mouths and dripping from our hair and it wasn't comfortable but it was more pleasing than gripping a podium or being dressed in an attire appointed by a

meaningless code. We had not chosen to be drenched and cold but we had placed ourselves within the elements, and that is very different than being forced into a safe and warm though numbing silence.

This didn't happen looking into AG's eyes (though maybe it did to a certain extent for H), but it came looking through his eyes at everyone and then through everyone's eyes until we were in between all of the eyes. It wasn't coupling but insisting on a group reaction. And then our group activity was a type of belonging others called thievery. We dared to claim our bodies, to use them, our thoughts as territory not possible to think of in terms of numbers, podiums, publicity or presentiment. And because we dared to do this we were outside certain fraught, though much coveted, aquariums. We could think in our own wet interiors. We had the rain and how it also drove the salt water back into our bodies. Of our own volition we befriended the

salt water. It clung to us and it hung in the air, an everpresent mist. All the while the podium clenchers and the ones who didn't want to know what we knew sat in their dry, plodding aquariums scoffing at our unkempt exteriors. It was the ocean which made me first consider tears as a chemical signaling vehicle to change. We owned our own tears and we might use them, not only to display our affinities but to galvanize empathy.

There were also the calculating hopefuls, whom we dubbed the 'determinants.' They were confused about the purpose of art. They would have never argued that the purpose was nothing, which made art more valuable by not being a commodity. Nor would they have argued that the purpose was to create any change or alterations to fraught and corrupt systems, or even to alter consciousness. What they wanted were the rewards of the questionable systems. The determinants wanted prizes, and because they defined their success upon their ability to win prizes they devised an elaborate system to aid them in this pursuit. They made spreadsheets to analyze the vocabulary in prize winning poems, the subject matter, the forms and lengths. They studied prize winning art and memorized the maxims of the judges of the prizewinners (who had of course been prize winners themselves). The thing that we could not understand was how the determinants could be at once both intelligent and also stupid. How could they possibly believe that the purpose of any creative act was to win? In learning to imitate a set of chosen prize winning practices, what had they become? The determinants clung to the institutions, adored the "insiders" and scoffed at the established non-establishment of the 'other possibles,' who themselves scoffed at the institutions, yet there was a way in which their own non-institutionalization had itself become an institution. We were as bothered by this as we were by the institutors themselves. We realized that we did not despise any of these structures, just how persons behaved within them in, in the names of them, or outside of them—as if architecture, or lack thereof, were a justification for snubbing, stabbing, pushing, breeching, limiting, harassing, enthroning, entombing, embalming, beheading, hitting on, neglecting, prevaricating, blaming or forgetting. It seemed that persons had borrowed semblances of themselves in order to permit certain tasks or avert their own catastrophes by enabling the catastrophes of others. If persons had not thought of themselves as machines they could not possibly have decided upon becoming one of the "determinants."

About this time I had a dream that I was at a literary function. I was at a large round table covered with white cloth and goblets of ice water beaded with condensation. The purpose of the function was to re-examine a set of parameters which had been set as criteria for judging a prestigious award. Everyone in the gigantic ballroom seated at similar tables had been given a sheet of paper which listed the current criteria. Our task was to revise and add to the criteria as we saw fit, and to submit our suggestions to the board. But no one was taking this task seriously. I'd never been to any literary events that even mildly resembled this. Everyone was waiting in their seats for the next course in an elaborate and elegant meal. I began to ignore the conversation around me, which seemed all about the imitation of art as industry. I wondered why I had been invited. I turned to read to the criteria in front of me. The first three were as follows:

1. The writer must be male.

2. The writer must be Caucasian.

3. The writer must have already been awarded prizes x, y & z.

I couldn't read any further. I looked up in panic. I stupidly assumed that no one else had read the criteria and I turned to the person closest to me and began to rave. Conversation stopped around me. I was trying to animate the group, saying, we must rewrite these criteria! Then I noticed that one man was eyeing me. He was the most famous and most celebrated writer of his generation. He had once held a prestigious chair at an elite University. He was white, middle-aged, and had been dead for at least a decade. He had been awarded prizes m through z. He said: *I wrote those criteria.*

When I finished relating this scenario I wanted to laugh but couldn't. HG was rapidly scribbling. What are you writing, O asked him. He then produced his own criteria, which O took up and began reading:

1. The writer must be alive.

2. The writer must have had no formal education.

3. The writer must be unemployed.

O stopped reading and said, why don't you add: The writer must demonstrate a bias against craft and comprehensibility?

HG replied, that's very good, and nodded encouragingly. Then he said, why don't you add: The writer must be difficult.

O asked, difficult in what way?

P asked why we didn't really write the criteria but O replied that the idea was abhorrent, the idea of a prize, of criteria, the banquet of privilege. We all agreed. But I was thinking also that P wanted to write the criteria for the book she wasn't writing. Maybe she just wanted to know what it was, if it were possible that such criteria could exist and not be objectionable.

AG suggested that what we might attempt would be to live the criteria (not assuming that we'd all have the same), which made sense because it would be reflected in everything we did. We would write it between ourselves—was the implication that encouraged and also tortured us because it is so easy to seem principled in isolation, to think and to write how things should be, to imagine the cellular change of the species, to feel falsely uplifted by some paltry effort and then to realize that writing a letter or showing up for an action can sometimes magnify all of the faults of everyone involved, or can have no effect whatsoever. We were trying to articulate that place which is not naïve sentimentalism or militant self-righteousness. It had to exist but we had yet to discover how to even begin to think about criteria for our lives and our work. I really did like O's assertion that the writer must be alive, so I brought that up as an initial point of exploration and AG responded by asking us what we thought that meant. We obviously agreed that we did not mean signs of life such as pulse or respiration but that it must have something to do with consciousness and action. We thought about how the first three horrid criteria in my dream had suggested other criteria such as conservative politics and a certain comfort level implying that the writer didn't need a large cash prize. This list went on and on until we realized that the point of the system in place was not to enable artists but to encourage a climate in which certain aesthetic practices were assumed.

I am merely a smudge of ash. Adamant, along the line of anyone's
lashes. Hands. Mouth. Impenetrable, something you crush between
your fingertips. The cold dregs of yesterday's hearth. A dark fomen-
tation, unyielding, someone to draw with, to mark the outlines of
afternoons. A cutting tool. All of my companions light me, decorate
my dark mask. It is their flare you see in the red of my lip, a loz-
enge-shaped figure on a playing card. It is their splash of color or blaze
of light which animates my diametrical opposites. I crumble. I stare. I
am so common but I carry with me a reliable line.

I say to P, if you are someone else today, this has perhaps nothing to do with your actions. She turns and smiles, then lays out a little wooden table for tea. NA has joined us. P has changed her mind about AG.

We sit in silence and when we finish P describes blankness.

AG says these are states which are not synonymous with our endeavor, but the usual impediments.

Not our scathes, P interrupts

Haunts, echoes AS.

AG smiles and continues. Yes, if there is still a mind to doubt—.

Which there must be, replies O, from his corner behind a book.

No, suggests H.

And the emptiness, asks P.

If you enter a place dark and indifferent, asks NA.

That would be ordinary, said AG.

AS is uninterested but he plays the part very well with one arm about her waist. P is now wading. Where once she was closed now she is curious. P believes now, as I have for some time, that AG can help with our unwritten plight. We have never been farther from naming it. Later, gazing at AG and P and AS quietly talking, I remember who it is I should appeal to for guidance. It is not the rain. It is not the rutted land. It is not in human speech or light or music, but possibly all of these things.

AG warns me, if you try on this insistent cloak of mourning you might find yourself adorned with never-ending flowers. NA calls them problematically fragrant. Is this where we wade, into such ridiculously pledged discourse? Who are we speaking of? We are still fictional versions of ourselves. We bend from the waist carefully and do not plunder or visit any acreage unwilling. I know not what I am saying. I have turned off all ancillary universes and can only hear the beckon of trodden heels. Oars upon water. Arms spread to night.

The storm welcomes us. Nothing happens in the story to help us claim the fictional status we covet. If I only look to the ground, no wonder. Your knee and my shoulder. I am merely C. If I look, I may be somewhere.

P scoffed at my public crying project but then she had no problem with displays of effusiveness. She also had all sympathy for my tears regarding the diagnosis of MG. I cried with NA about P and AS, and about H and AG, my secret scathes, even though I suspected that I'd only desired him as an idea. Ironically, at this moment fraught with suppressed tears, P decided to be a subject in a psychological study on crying and this reinforced my desire to explore public crying as a project. I learned that crying may serve as a chemical signaling function and that men in the study who sniffed women's tears had reduced levels of testosterone. This was linked to less sexual arousal and also to less violence. I began haphazard research on the history of crying and kept an archive of notes on the subject. What is the relation between the book one does not write—the hypothetical—at which we fail by omission—and the tears we do not release? Can language replace tears? Or the sentence in a dream one cannot recall? I include an excerpt here from my archive:

Lacrimation

Of a mournful character, water from the eye. I thought I was reading an imagined book to read the unwritten.

What silent crested drops are those from embryonic?

Tear, from earlier teahor, tæhhertakh, tagr. So many times I look at the surface and cannot—.

In the animal world, maxillary and frontonasal prominences appear. A sentence. From which lacrimal book?

From Latin, lacrima, dacrima, dakrym.

The modern verb is lacrimation. You have to want to look at the cover even to open it.

Tear gas first recorded 1917, nor precious drops are those.

An inscription of tears was found upon the oldest woven cloth.

A specific act associated with trickling, considered by many cultures as infantile.

"The silver key of the fountain of tears" (Shelley).

Blind mole rats rub tears on their bodies to keep aggressive mole rats away.

Professional or paid mourning is a mostly historical occupation practiced in Near Eastern cultures and many other parts of the world.

The lacrimal sac sits within the lacrimal fossa, so that exclusion wasn't what it seemed.

Even the non-living and the uncertainty that surrounds the future are bound anteriorly by the frontal process of the maxillary bone.

Cough-like, convulsive breathing, sometimes involving spasms of the whole upper body. Will we be loved?

Tear-jerker is attested from 1921, on model of soda jerker.

Coating the outer surface of light constricting apparatus is a "pre-lens tear film."

We meaning 'we" in the royal sense, or "we" as in the species.

We blink our eyelids every six seconds to replenish the film. We watch through a minute lake.

"No radiant pearl, which crested Fortune wears" (Erasmus Darwin).

Components of a tear film's 'skin': soap-like molecules. With water-soluble 'head' and insoluble 'tail,'

Paired almond-shaped glands, one for each eye, that secrete the aqueous layer of the tear film, we were insoluble, situated in the upper, outer portion of each orbit. Unencumbered we could simply invent.

Dakryein "to shed tears" with such lustre.

Emotional tears contain more of the protein-based hormones prolactin (natural painkillers) than basal or reflex tears.

At some point we were not allowed to interrupt our own births.

From dakry "tear" we open or tear the pages of the book.

"What I should say

My tears gainsay; for every word I speak,

Ye see, I drink the water of mine eyes."(Shakespeare, Henry VI, Part III (c. 1591), Act V, scene 4, line 73.)

A sentence could never explain and yet this sentence did.

If the eye's tears are "isotonic," there will be no change in water volume and vision will remain normal. If the tears are "hypotonic," water will flow into the cornea (such as when crying or swimming in a pool) and it will swell, causing it to become more myopic. If the tears are "hypertonic," water will flow out of the cornea (such as when swimming in the ocean) and it will shrink, causing it to become more hyperopic.

Of course I cannot remember the sentence whether swimming or no.

Puncta are directed posteriorly against the globe; therefore, they are not usually visible unless the eyelid is everted.

What I do remember is the enormous relief of putting down entire structures of thought and that epiphora is overflow of tears onto the face.

"Tears are sometimes as weighty as words" (Ovid).

The liquid film has a protective coating just one or two molecules thick, rather like the surface of an elusive sentence.

A lightness revealed itself and that lightness could coincide with your body.

We live in three layers with aqueous being our center.

Some other constituents of sentence films are hydrophobic- fearful of the tears enabling their composition.

Our tears have four main functions:

Lubricating our oracular instruments.

Creating a smooth optical surface on the front of the irregular political surface.

Acting as the main supplier of oxygen to alphabetic utterances.

Preventing the growth of prevaricating cysts on our syntactical enclave.

The epithelial surface of the cornea is naturally "hydrophobic" (water-repelling). For a text layer to remain on the surface without rolling off, the "hydrophilic" (water-attracting) layer of the text film is laid down onto the surface of thought by "goblet cells." In turn, the lacrimal layer of the sentence film can defy gravity and remain on the front of the eye.

"For a tear is an intellectual thing" (William Blake).

The lacrimal lake is the pool of tears, vernal morn.

I wrote this sentence repeatedly but each time I was required to remove all evidence of doing so, flushing harmful contaminants from our vision, into the lacrimal canals and out through the nose.

Bouncing X-rays off the surface of both the natural and artificial sentence analogues composed of a comparable mixture of utterances showed that in both the real and the synthetic sentence, words seem to line up in regular, orderly arrays, rather like two-dimensional crystals.

When researchers added fluorescent molecules to synthetic sentence films containing just recalled components, they saw that the letters separated into two different states: a relatively disorderly two-dimensional liquid, and a more closely packed, crystal-like state. Lettered crystals grew into remarkable patterns shaped rather like flower heads.

This arrangement enables the sentence film to keep a relatively constant structure even when it is severely squeezed and stretched, as is likely to happen for example when we blink: squeeze the film and the lettered crystals grow a bit bigger; stretch it out and they become smaller again.

"My words are my tears" (Beckett).

When I am finished with the blue arch book I will open it and begin again.

About this time two terrible things happened. The first was the phone call about MG having seizures and brain swelling and rushing to the emergency room. I was then on a plane and in the kind of shock that illustrates clearly that anyone's notions can change in an instant. You can walk into a room and utter a simple sentence and a world is gone. AG explained: your regard for me is conditional, meaning that if I am horrid you won't love me. He did not say this to me in particular, but to an audience, in a talk. Everyone heard his statement as if it were addressed to them individually. O was suspicious of AG's abilities, but P and H and HG and even S and AS all felt that he wasn't false or even allotropic. H called him *garnet, place, haunt.*

I rushed between airports to visit MG. I was sure at this point that I could have been a subject in the psychological crying study because they had a hard time finding anyone who could cry enough tears. My new realization that a simple sentence could change anyone held me up as I made endless phone calls and requested information from hospital staff and home health workers about the details of medication and treatment schedules.

As I was returning home the second horrible thing happened. The phone call from P about the bullet through the brain of the protester, the politician, the witness, the bystander. The man profiled in today's paper was shot seven times, including once in the head, and survived. A demonstrator waves a banner as rubbish burns. A woman near the attacker was on the ground and she grabbed his gun while he was trying to reload. Nearly two-hundred people had been arrested in the park and fifty or sixty in the streets nearby. Two men tackled the suspect. A young man rushed to the one hit then organized triage on the others. He lifted her up, cleared her airway, applied pressure to the wound. On one side of a barrier police—bodies lined up, clutching sticks. On the other an embrace between a tattooed forearm, a baseball cap with red star and gingham-clad layered figure with a gawking mask on the back of their head. On one side riot gear, tear gas, bean bag bullets and other projectiles. On the other side a protester occupies a tree before the eviction. On one side protesters argued that the shooting was not connected to the sit-in and on the other side laws banning open fires, overnight camping in public and the use of propane. The desire to occupy everything with mass non-violent action drew us away from other thoughts and actions until a numbness began to counter the myriad images, which became, eventually, like precipitation—a cold sheet obscuring the final weight of any one image. On one side was the persistent or obsessive consumption of the images, sleeplessness. On the other side—paralysis. We wondered how much blankness we must draw up around ourselves before we might insert a thought palace. We wondered how to collect ourselves—our reservations as well as our probable actions.

No one wanted to talk about it and everyone could talk about nothing else. On everyone's lips was the repetition of a series of violent actions which we could not comprehend. When we turned on the radio or searched the news the same series of events was reported. The expressions of the commentators and reporters varied every time, as if what they were repeating were urgent utterances not yet heard. We listened tensely, waiting for something, and still responding to the briefings as if they were new. Then we went about repeating the utterances. Our phones rang, and faraway friends asked us to repeat the series of actions again.

When the events occurred I was in the hospital with MG. She was almost ready to leave and we were helping her dress when the phone rang. The phone continued to ring as she was wheeled to the parking lot, as we finished with the last flurry of forms. Later when I picked up the message I was driving to get her meds at the pharmacy. P's voice related the series of actions. I will not repeat them because they are so well known. You have only to remember the media repeating any calamity non-stop, with no additional information. The same swelling will arise as you raise a hand to your throat, the same disbelief possibly.

I kept thinking about the chemical signaling in tears and how one of the researchers had called it a type of language. How might a sentence of tears work as a remedy to violence? Vigils were going on at this time. I thought about collecting a tear bank to be used in future, dribbled down the cheeks of young men before entering airports or political gatherings, but I later learned that the tears had to be fresh, cried within two to three hours. I wanted to create an action around tear collection. I wanted everyone to recover, but mostly I wanted to understand the possibilities of persuasion and to find ways to enable them as alternatives to violence.

I proposed that we perform a public action of crying and a tear collection bank. HG and O claimed they lacked the capacity for tears. This didn't surprise me. In the study that P had been in, experiments were conducted with 114 subjects, all of them female. The donor women in the study, including P, watched sad film-clips in isolation, and used a mirror and vial to capture tears. The researchers estimated that if they had relied on men's tears the study would have taken several years longer to complete. HG, S, O, AG, and later AS agreed to collect the tears and help to distribute them. This was, however, after much dispute in which I, NA, P and H tried to persuade them to be criers as well. We argued that it did not matter if they were not as prolific. We wanted to know about the chemical signaling in men's tears, and also we wanted to see them cry because we wanted to share this public action as fully as we could. But in the end after several practice sessions in which the men (except S, who was our sole male sobber) produced nothing, we dubbed them pathetic, dismissed them as criers, and moved forward with our plan.

I talked to MG daily. When sickness is no longer visible it moves inside to deeper recesses available to only the one who is ill. The most we can do is commit to seeing the unseeable, an empathy worn across the waist, hoisted over a shoulder, dabbed in the corners of the eyes and touched to the voice. All at once then I found myself in her rooms again. I have no memory of days or weeks and I could not tell you how long it had been since my previous visit. I threw off my coat, sat beside her and took her hands. She was angry about the invisibility of non-violent protest in the media, the idiocy of firearm legislation. I had told her about the public crying project and she was taking notes for an essay she was writing on the subject. I saw her tentative title was "At War with Invisibles, the Practice of Seething." Seething is almost seeing plus "th" is almost "the." How two letters make a difference. This was not unrelated to practices of counting letters to access meaning using sacred mathematics, which was one of her areas of scholarly expertise. She was well enough to inscribe our war, to help us with the project of visibility. We had seethed plenty.

Once I was back again and working on our public crying project I wanted to know why no discriminations are made between those who are apt and able, those who have adequate cause, and those who, being young and of unsound mind, are able to go into a shop and purchase a gun.

P interrupted me and picked up the page I was reading. She walked across the room and found a marker. Then she proceeded cross out the word "magazine" and other words referring to "firearms" throughout the piece and to replace them with the word 'mind.' She said, minds have been replaced by guns. She handed the paper back to me, and I read:

> *The detachable mind is often mistakenly referred to as a clip; such usage is sometimes frowned upon by authorities but is nonetheless commonplace. Minds come in many shapes and sizes, from bolt action express minds that hold only a few rounds to machine minds that hold hundreds. Since the mind is an essential part of most repeating fire-minds, they are often subject to regulation by mind control laws seeking to limit the number of minds they hold. The first mind fed fire-mind*

to achieve widespread success was the Spencer repeating mind, which saw service in the American Civil War. Upon inserting a loaded mind the user depresses the slide stop, throwing the slide forward, stripping a round from the top of the mind stack and chambering it. In single-action minds this action keeps the hammer cocked back as the new round is chambered, keeping the mind ready to begin firing again.

I was surprised to learn that guns are permitted almost everywhere in many states except a business or doctor's office. The state rifle association lists restaurants that permit concealed weapons. Guns are permissible inside the state Capitol and many other public buildings. State law permits gun owners to carry a concealed weapon into establishments that serve alcohol as long as the gun owner isn't imbibing. Concealed guns are permitted on school grounds while picking up or dropping off a child, as long as the weapon is unloaded and remains in a vehicle. If you cast your ballot in a church, fire station or municipal building, you may carry a gun with you.

O told us about a student. She had a face like stone, painted red lips and such exaggerated facial expressions that you knew something was wrong. You wished there were not. She was otherwise harmless. She isn't anyone you've ever met but you know her, elementally in the way she leans on her elbow and madly scribbles adjusting the metal grommets at her waist and wrists. Her initials are LI and before the class is halfway through she has spoken of her instability. But you knew before she even spoke, her features begging attention.

You cannot imagine how many students approach his desk and look into O's complexion as if to ask, may I enter? O always keeps his writing utensils in a particular arrangement that forms a symbolic barrier. We all laughed when we first realized this, but he insists that this array, which he never fails to present, stops the pressing students for a moment, long enough for them to think he might be too orderly or OCD to be sympathetic. They take it as a warning.

The array of implements, now also more strange than when he began this display ritual, is ridiculously outdated. Mechanical pencils and erasers are still perhaps useful. Though the sheer number of them, along with calculators, mini-stapler, and protractor, form an odd installation, especially to students who assume them to be incongruous with courses in philosophy. The display gives them pause, which also allows O time to prepare a response. He could typically tell which kind of question it would be. There were those with questions whose answers were obvious and annoyingly things the students should have known, had they given any amount of attention to the course. These were the most common. Then there were the questions about missed classes and missed assignments. And he would count the dead grandmothers (the ones who only died at midterms or finals week) on his toes. A student once told him that he missed class because he had been unconscious. That was his favorite excuse until he later learned that the student had mental health issues and had been found in his dorm room, barely in time, and yet still refused counseling.

But the point of his telling had been centered around this one student and what she represented to him—a psychic silence that proceeds by yelling and tripping across its own perimeters. There is no avoiding the gaze, though one may try. And that is the story of how LI became involved in our Tears for Non-Violent Protest project (TFNVP), sometimes referred to as Collective Tears Project (CLP) or Public Crying Project (PCP). We never did agree what to call ourselves. LI arrived, in tall black boots laced up to her thighs, a corset and gobs of black eyeliner smudged to her cheekbones. We were all afraid of her actually, because one had the sense that she might cry at any moment. She could be brought to tears easily and brought others to tears expertly and repeatedly. We were surprised at how useful she became. Her youth and dramatic appearance made her a visible magnet for attracting participants. She was to receive class credit for her work with us. O avoided her as much as possible. She immediately bonded with H, which surprised none of us.

We stumbled along our collective process to protest arguing amongst ourselves; for instance, HG looked at us a bit venomously but we were used to his "bookings" as he called them.

Oh, he would say, you've definitely earned it. A summary of your reservation has been sent. He knew that we weren't to be congratulated. He liked to talk about how we had to rebook ourselves into everyday reality. How nothing is automatically returned to our accounts, as if we had any accounts with him. But we did because he said so. And we were all okay with this. When things went awry we were told to review our trip details. And that's how we knew we had been anywhere or were about to depart. And because we couldn't afford to travel much it worked for us to be a part of this ongoing simulation. We were very self-reliant in this way. No one else knew and we felt privileged considering that the Insiders and the Other Possibles and the Determinants could only go somewhere on an expense account or a grant or an invitation.

HG was stringing us along today. He kept repeating the word "eviscerated" as if it meant everything. He picked up Bolaño and read aloud his own version: "*I am eviscerated now, but I still have many things to eviscerate. I used to be eviscerated with myself. Quiet and eviscerated. But it all blew eviscerated quite unexpectedly.*"

O gave him a scathing look. I could tell that H was about to bolt up from her chair and intervene but then HG's look softened and he said, still holding the Bolaño, *that wizened youth is eviscerated.* O squinted as if to better understand his meaning and HG put down the book. Then HG offered helpfully, I'm just translating you know, and this text has already been translated at least once. I'm translating into this eviscerated moment.

O asked what was so very eviscerated about it? We all wished simultaneously that O had not asked this question, because we knew that HG had been compulsively reading everything regarding the shooting and subsequent legislation in process which would enable the carrying of guns onto school campuses. This was just HG's way of parading a particular brand of discontent. He had many modes of discontent, and our "bookings" or evisceration seemed pleasantly mild, relatively speaking, and so I knew that we all simultaneously had wished because when this happens the old glass in the parlour window shudders. We call it a parlour only because the glass is old and wavy, and we imagine we might have fine times in a parlour. When we heard the glass vibrating it was obvious that our wish worked because HG began again with his etymological pacing, which is always a sign that he is moving slowly downward, descending whatever peak of "bookings" we had been given.

He began: abate, 1620s, attenuate, from Latin evisceratus, to disembowel. Blunt, from ex- out + viscera internal organs. Cramp, cripple—sometimes used 17c. in figurative sense, dampen, deaden, debilitate. To bring out the deepest (devitalize, draw, enfeeble) secrets of. Exhaust, extenuate, gruel, gut. Related: Eviscerated; eviscerating. Lay low, mitigate, rattle, sap, shake, unbrace, unstring, weaken.

When he had finished with this list he sat and lifted his hands to his face and began to rub. H sat beside him. She didn't say a word, but he soon began to talk about the Insiders and the Other Possibles and the Determinants and she asked what about them, before he could add to his list of miserables. What about them, he repeated indignantly and we all feared we were about to be booking again. But then noting our attention he softened slightly and began to speak as if we were actually persons.

There had been an icy undone shoulder at the Institute where he had had some meeting or other to attend to a young writer who wanted to know more about his poem which mused largely upon Jupiter, fulminations, oak cleaving and sheet lightning. It had been published by a local micro press and carefully sewn in a very small number, yet it was superior in every way to many of the very flashy, shiny, and perfect bound covers among which it was carelessly nestled. He had gone and after his highly enjoyable interview several icy shoulders had walked by and definitively had not said hello to him. The breadth of the ice upon the shoulders was unbelievable. It was as if everyone were wearing large mantles of icy armor, as upon royalty with epaulets.

What he had done to inspire such treatment was in question. H interrupted and said that it was unfathomable because it was unknowable and it was unknowable because the Insiders didn't know themselves. It was just their general practice to go around wearing such junk. Though it must be cold and uncomfortable. H looked a bit worried as she said this, as if their gleaming mantles might be the cause of coldness, upper respiratory infections or even exhaustion and therefore poor decision making. O broke in and said that it must be in the job description to have to wear such frigid glossy mantles, and what sort of booking had HG expected? Why did he choose to meet the young writer in the Institute? They could have met anywhere. This was true, but it was also true that we did all want to be as near to the books as possible. We longed for all of the books, the small and lavishly stitched as well as the glossy tomes and small straight spines all lined up as if in an apothecary, even if it did mean risking the brush of the icy mantle. This was all the backdrop or the backroom or the drop-out fade in accounting for how HG had come to choose "eviscerate" as his word of the day. There was behind this rancid tale that of the shooting and whatever was in the papers today besides. I for one had not dared to look.

It seems that we are always in each other's company, an elemental band which manages to move through time in unison. Or maybe only those times in company are worth remembering, and so everything else drops away, is forgotten in a large undocumented expanse. Do we stand in each other's tiny kitchens night after night? Possibly we live in different parts of town. In different states and time zones. We might have fallen away from one another and now rarely speak. Or speak different languages. We met at a bar or a public event only once. All of us are fictional.

I say this to P once and she calls me a liar. Then she asks me to leave; she is expecting AS. I grab my coat and stand, searching for keys and shoes. If I had invented these companions I would not always have made it winter. I might have made them a bit more predictable or even kind. But P isn't listening. She swirls a dress over her head and tugs at a zipper at the base of her spine. She squints into a mirror with an expression I'd call dismissive—not to her reflection, but to my voice. As if my voice isn't happening. On the stairs on the way down I pass AS on his way up. He is smiling at me because he can see that I'm leaving. From the problematic perspective of descending any flight of stairs there is the unfortunate question of where one is going. Also, what has been forgotten five flights up when one cannot go back. Or at least that is the way it seems after having carried one's body such a distance. The physical distance is one thing and the distance from the dismissive expression examining itself in a mirror is another.

When we are all assembled in memory I ask myself why it takes so long to compose a paragraph but O says it is because we have to be able to comfortably inhabit that space. He isn't talking about reclining or tromping about but the physical sensation of words falling out of the mouth, off of the fingers. He says this very confidently, as if he has spoken of himself as made up of characters of an alphabet as long as he can remember. He also asserts that time and dialogue confine us to such a space, but HG disagrees and H looks rather uncomfortable but says nothing for a time. Finally she gets up and interrupts the bantering between O and HG and tells us all that we shouldn't think in terms of solidity of bodies or of space but of the fluidity necessary in order to move. She looks over to AG, who takes her hand quickly and retreats. P continues to scoff at her reflection in my memory, though this couldn't be true for this scene. I think it is because she strongly dislikes the idea of existing in a text, in black and white. So she vanishes, or finds some other way to leave—someone walking away from her, usually me.

What we wished for was not to be driven away to a point beyond the horizon where we lay back sleepy and satisfied. What we wished for was to be awake. We wanted to find a way to direct our tears to some useful means beyond falling slowly down our cheeks to our jaws, beyond dropping onto our necks and upon the shoulders of those to whom we cried. To be told that our tears were looking glasses was not helpful. We did not tilt our wet faces up to the light expectantly.

To cry in public openly and without apology is to undermine shame. But sentiment, among many thinkers, plotters, "insiders" and "other possibles," is regarded with suspicion as a type of sediment. We were not willing to be gravel but hoarsely we interjected our hopes as if incrementally we could shift the terrifying fabric of nullification.

The voices which did not speak and the bodies which did not move made up what we called the terrifying fabric. O came up with this term because of our ongoing argument about institutions. Is it the persons in and around and outside the institution that are problematic, or is it the thing itself? But the thing itself, P argued, is inanimate. How can we fear it? The sheer weight of it was paralyzing but it did not exist without us. The fabric was our composite weight and represented something used to sheathe anyone trying to look at a thing itself.

Everyone involved creates a portion of the terrifying fabric simply by breathing nearby, entering its premises or thinking. If you were to collect all of this weaving of thought you'd have a two-dimensional sheathe. The reason it is terrifying is that it seems that we unconsciously though deliberately use the fabric as an excuse to know nothing. We wrap it around ourselves and retreat to a corner. We cover our heads and drop.

P kept writing in fits and not in any order at all. She called her process spasmodically arranged. Not knowing how to proceed in planning our public crying project, I continued to take notes in my messy archive. One impediment we considered was the difficulty of eliciting tears. In response I created these prompts:

How to Cry:

1. *I forgot how to cry*— is a common complaint. First, read the news, for example, Man who tied up toddlers to watch sports at a bar gets prison term, Las Vegas, 1 hour ago. Binding, gagging, tying the boys to chairs in a garage.

2. Drink lots of liquids. How long can you survive on beer alone? Heat stress can be a problem for calves that dissipate heat by panting. Donate water to the homeless.

3. Keep your eyes open. Don't confine your experience to what you can fit on a piece of paper. Expose your eyes to as much air as possible. Try to prop eyes open for two minutes.

4. Think of something sad. Wiesel notes the celebrations that attended the killing of bin Laden and that normally he 'would respond to such scenes with deep apprehension. The execution of a human being - any human being - should never be an event to be celebrated.'

5. Cut an onion. Advocates are digesting the various proposals contained in the Senate budget. Peeling back the layers.

6. Hurt yourself. Slam your nose in the freezer door. Collide. Inhale something toxic. Burn or scald. Fall down stairs. Rusty cutting implements. Electrocution. Slip or trip.

7. Watch a sad movie. Born into Brothels. Fans cry foul over panhandling dog at NYC stadiums.

8. Relax your facial muscles. Put down your smartphone. Ontario to relax liquor laws by summer.

We considered this list as a handout to newcomers. We began arguing over vials and containment. We began discussing a strategic plan to disperse ourselves in the public square. We read the news with an eye toward locations and events that might lend themselves to our undertaking. H wondered if there were a way that we could invoke spontaneous crying in a crowd, thus avoiding the need to collect tears in the first place. Her thought was that we could enlist individuals present an hour or so before the event—both to donate tears and also to encourage crying among others. We designed ways to use social media to coordinate similar events in other cities simultaneously, and also to upload a video clip to hand held devices which would induce crying. But what video clip would most induce crying? We searched and found various irrelevant suggestions. Fake criers. Then we discovered a whole blog for people who can't stop crying in public. HG's unsympathetic advice to the OMG-I-can't-stop-crying crowd: Stop going out in public.

We had all of the pieces, we thought, to create this event, and yet we did not know how to assemble them, almost as if we could create a shape with our bodies if we could be free of gravity. Individuality was problematic, even between us, because we had too many perspectives to mesh and we had never before collaborated on such a scale. I imagined a long process which would, through time and pressure, amount to a modest though lucid crystallization of actions. P imagined another scenario entirely, one that congealed quickly and exploded dramatically. H was patient and thoughtful though not at all expressive about how to proceed. She could stand atop a public fountain and cry indefinitely with no detailed plan but to observe. AS had no interest in a sustained effort, his only motive being the elusive P. O and HG were engaged in continual bantering which often became so tangential to our aspirations that it seemed our pace would never quicken. I saw them within a perpetual set of parentheses going at it at with undue speed and volume. Sometimes LI entered the debates and could not stop talking. Other times she said little, and instead sat in a corner to practice crying. S tried to mediate until it became clear that this might be the problem. Still, we plodded along.

In preparation for our public action we attempted to ritually and collectively address our inadequacies and in some ways it was easier to do this together, in terms of finding each other's blind spots. But we were prone to argue, each of us ready to offer up what we believed to be our worst tendencies. When we presented them though, like sore talents, the others of us would most likely laugh. We were more foolish than we could ever have imagined, like animals showing a spot with no fur, turning around to show dirt, remnants of gnawing and tracings of blame. After prolonged exposure to mental groping we were hesitant and we tried to walk out of the circle, but that wasn't allowed. We'd unintentionally found a new way to produce tears. In our hurry to be through with the process, in our good opinions of ourselves, and in our self-delusion, we all assumed that we were giving up our most difficult relics: a tongued pleasure at someone's loss, a desire to touch indiscriminately, without thought, and yet when it came down to it our first representations of weaknesses were nothing more than screens carefully adjusted so as to make a scene bearable to ourselves. We knew each other better than we knew ourselves and for this reason we could torture each other lovingly and without trying too hard. Usually this could happen without any words. We emptied our pockets and I cannot even describe what was placed on the table in these evenings. Scratches, blemished hand held retrievals, stolen articles of time, garments of continuous nodding sleep. But these were just props to stand in for words. The unnamable place was somewhere here, not in this location, but between our bodies, in this process of renaming what we hoped to forge. We didn't know what to call ourselves anymore. We were all each other. At least that seemed to make the process more democratic. So we adopted a policy that in confession we must all take on the name of the one who came offering, and this unanimous naming continued until we had finished.

We were forbidden to record or repeat anything that occurred during these sessions, and therefore I cannot reproduce any of them here. In place of a transcript is a text that P and I composed together— a fictional account of U:

U entered the circle in a metallic grey raincoat. He picked up a glass which appeared yellow-green in the light. He looked very hot but he kept on his coat. He opened his hand and offered to us something we could not see. We asked him what it was and he said that he needed to cast off. His brief half-life was exposed. We did not laugh because we all knew U could easily split. Yielding like an emotive environmental problem he could spill, contaminate. He was so dense and weighty he seemed to be the opposite of H, who stood far off at the other side of the room. U could generate a plethora of energy, express an enormous influence. In the end we had to reveal him to himself through pantomime. What he needed was to find a way to contain himself. He needed to impossibly float. His tone could be corrosive but he listened and was malleable. A layer of doubt seemed to cover his skin. Finally, after bearing our scorn for what seemed an indefinite period of time, he lay down on the table, asked for a brush and began scrubbing at the metallic layer which clung to his skin.

It sounded ludicrous with all of us addressing each other by one name. Eye contact and tonal emphasis became crucial in making ourselves clear. Our collective pronouncements were the end or beginning of something not at all sought, a ribbon, written in fits and prompts. We tried to forgive ourselves through forgiving each other. We could often not find the floor. We knew that it was untruthful to think that through a series of ritualized disclosures we would be any better equipped to pull off what we considered to be an apocalyptic action—if not shattering to those around us, then to our own molecular structures at least. We knew we had become victims of our habits of speech and silence so we played a game to undermine our rhetorical dynamics. We shuffled some cards and handed them out before we began. Whoever had the floor was "It." Everyone else was a Player. "It" would begin by downloading, unveiling, or performing. Then the players would respond in turn. One player, the Listener, was forbidden to speak and served as scribe. The Detractor could only speak in constructive criticism. The Speaker could comment after any comment by anyone, and balance the Detractor. The Extoller could only speak in praise and the Inquirer could only speak in questions.

We liked the term Player because it reminded us that if we were not playing in our efforts there was no reason to continue. Since we addressed each other all by the same name, this erased the notion that any of us were anyone. In other words if S were confessing, then the Detractor, the Speaker, the Inquirer, the Extoller, and the Listener were all S. This would help "It" not to isolate or empathetically separate from the process. We called this process our Jam because it was a type of discordant music and though none of us were musical we all secretly wished to be but only in a way that would make everyone uncomfortable.

One evening during our Jam something peculiar happened, and as I am sworn not to say whose Jam it was, and since in fact each one belonged to all of us, I'll simply say X, and invent everything.

What occurred was a collective listing of ailments, griefs confessions, maelstroms, and finally premonitions.

We often wondered in all of this mess what we were guilty of and why it was so difficult to empty our attributes—which seemed indistinguishable from a slimy mess of aquatic weeds. They clung. Was it that simply in accumulating a number of years there was an unquestionable facet through which everything looked uncertain? Was it that while we were busy occupying ourselves with various pursuits, others, not chosen, welled up awkward and distended? X recalled a statement from his young nephew, 'what's the difference between growing up and throwing up?' This made us laugh but only momentarily because X worried why a young boy would think such a thing. Please recall that at this point in the narrative, everyone is X. Then X said that the young boy probably made this statement accidentally, at which point X said that that was near to impossible. X corrected X by saying what X meant was that the child had made a connection between *growing* and *throwing* and this possibly had to do purely with sound. Immediately X claimed to be guilty of assuming something about children and something about sound. Additionally X was guilty of neglecting to do anything about global warming. X was inactive in countering genocide. X did nothing to mollify toxicity in our water systems. X did not advocate against domestic abuse, violent communication, and the state of our public educational system. X was, however, solely dedicated to stopping violence in prisons through the development of a new technology that would enable inmates and staff to detect pheromones. Thus, X in mid-confession had unknowingly galvanized our Crying Project. Detecting a pheromone is somewhat analogous to chemical signaling in tears. But we did not stop here.

A longer list of collective confessions emerged including: It's not enough for us to read someone's stories; we also have to turn them into our own. We use our laptops for warmth. We're living in a culture that has oversimplified complex equations. Conversational narcissism. We took ourselves seriously. We were also removed nearly every day for interrupting testimony. We couldn't afford any of the gadgets we enjoy if laborers weren't willing to spend 12 hours a day producing them, in reportedly brutal conditions. We're all guilty in iPad suicides. A couple of technical infringements. I would not say this research provided no social value, but we have carried on an entire conversation with co-workers without even glancing up from our screens.

We decided to act on what we already knew, that a type of faith in what we could possibly do was not enough, that our bodies had to be implicated, included, not separated from any action.

The next day we were sitting together in yet another public square and any excuse will do for P to get up and walk away. Maybe that's why there are so many lonely activists. We could be lonely in a group, and when one of us got up, as P had just done, all we could do was to follow. AS got up. The ground beneath our feet was stone. Everyone stared at P as she walked, tilting a little to each side and occasionally looking over her shoulder. There were many people and the ground was so cold it felt almost hot. No one was using this public space. It was a perfect container. The buildings on each side were steel gray and imposing. A fountain in the center could be used as a focal point. At this moment the fountain was covered with persons clutching phones and skateboards. The walls were lined with flags, posters, plants and at one far end, a series of dull gray tents. Kids were carrying high tech camping gear. The sounds in the square were continuous.

Later that same day, happily caffeinated, we returned home. P said she didn't have time to read all of the books we had gathered. She dropped an armload of revolutionary titles onto the table. We read Gene Sharp's *From Dictatorship to Democracy* and made lists from his first appendix of methods of non-violent protest. The appendix contains one-hundred and ninety-eight methods. We'd never imagined so many. We chose several to incorporate in our collective act. We began with public speeches and statements. We made signs and banners with images of human tears. The next day we began preliminary actions. We went to the public square and one of us stood on the edge of the fountain and said something. Whether or not we were prepared to say anything it seemed very bold or possibly stupid to stand on the edge of a fountain. H wasn't interested in holding a banner or signing petitions but she did like to stand at the highest precipice on the fountain, in the central ring, and she gazed out at everyone and people gazed back. After practicing this on several occasions H asked us all to abandon our signage and to stand beside her and cry. LI joined her without hesitation and NA followed. HG and O laughed and said nothing. They devised faux petitions and mock elections for the role of Cry Leader. They convinced P to be their candidate and she wore a rhinestone tiara and her yellow dress. On our first attempt the faux petition said, *sign here, if you believe in chemical signaling and support collection of human tears for a public art protest.* In a few days we had gathered hundreds of signatures. We developed a database so that we would be ready to collect the actual tears at a later date. We wondered how many persons would show up and considered incentives we could offer. We couldn't pay so we needed the kind of sloganeering that someone in advertising or politics could muster. We knew that we lacked the proper skill sets to devise these statements ourselves; nevertheless we began and hoped that the sheer weight of our desire would count. We came up with Tears Against Violence, and Send a Chemical Signal for Change. We read *Cry, the Beloved Country.* We watched the film *Cry-Baby.* We studied the crystalline structure of water and salt. We imagined a public bath made from human tears. We imagined the public fountain as a fountain of literal tears and wondered how passersby would react. Would they note any difference? We set up two small containers, one with ordinary salt water and one with tears. In the public square, while standing in close proximity to the containers, held just under the chin, we asked participants to gaze into the unmarked containers and did a double blind study composed of a series of questions which tested levels of violent impulse which we correlated with levels of testosterone. We wrote up possible scenarios to reduce tendencies to violence in dangerous situations; for instance, in our airport experiment, participants occupying a terminal could arrest the violent impulses of a suicide bomber by crying upon command. Surrounded by hundreds of crying individuals, in each instance the suicide bomber would leave the premises, detach himself from the explosives and dismantle them. We imagined the implications of this action if globally persons were trained to cry upon command. In combat, in demonstrations, in the wake of natural disasters, violence, looting and damage could be avoided. We realized that we were ludicrously projecting, and yet crying seemed a skill all were capable of, and with a small amount of training this skill had potentially staggering possibilities. This of course seemed ironic to us, the generally marginalized and cynical, but the notion fit in perfectly with the model of society in which we lived, in which free and harmless resources were often ignored, slandered or denied.

In our actions we are beyond the believable and we divine, through tea leaves or wind, chemical signals, market rates or text codes of our clan—where we are driven next— furthest from before. Join our little gathering despite these many faults and without which we wonder whose art is reverential. Meet our misshapen family. This doesn't tell us who we are. So we had better get started with our day. We post our whereabouts and disappear like a spectrum walking, stick figures drowned green and dark faded. This image of us, arms linked, ambling away. The body reverts, reinvents.

AG sees us before we arrive and yells happily through handfuls of thyme and pomegranate. We are coming over for dinner, despite the quiet I'd prefer. And yet quiet would now be incomplete, too secret, like the letter "e" left off of particular words such as lit, bit, nil and far.

What about everyone's occupations- do we now more fully return to them? It shouldn't matter. Why would anyone want to know? Because, interrupts HG, everyone self identifies with what they do. But that has no place in P's novel. Especially in that chapter where all of us are X. H says that is how all of the chapters should be written and all of our days spent, all of us remaining X. AG gives her an admiring look, which she does not notice. She continues to say that if we could do that we wouldn't need to induce tears.

O is a philosopher and what that means is anyone's guess, except that he loves to argue. H loves everyone. HG is always changing his mind. A certain amount of patience is required. P is a chemical engineer. I like to draw. None of this belongs. We are going to have a little gathering. You are just entering our patch of concatenations. This little time of ours is sheerly nothing, loosely fitting. S says P should write it backwards and in pieces and in any way except forward and continuously. Periodically, P looks up from her desk but mostly ignores the banter. The reason anyone creates characters, she says, is for a particular type of company in which we give up the idea of control.

I have an indelible image of P in her lemon dress, standing on the edge of the fountain, tears streaming down her face, surrounded on all sides. There was finally, at this moment, no need to cry. But she was gleaming with wet cheeks and she did not attempt to wipe them away. P had rarely been able to summon tears, only fury and revamptive action. She did not cry when AS disappeared and she did not cry over MG's illness. P did not cry the night she was "It" and I believe she might have been the only one of us to withstand the prodding. All of her blunders were so starkly visible to everyone and yet she was not apologetic. The lemon dress reminds me of the dress of a doll I had as a child. She had delicately painted curls, plastic blue eyes with thick, still, black lashes. Her eyes did not close when she reclined. The dress was poplin yellow with tiny white dots. She smelled of apple juice and was my constant companion until she was buried in a closet. When I did remember her I dug her out, pulled her dress back down over her head and told her I was sorry. I was devastated by my own capacity for neglect.

The lemon dress was nothing like that actually, so it must have been that I wanted to pull P out of something, smooth her dress, apologize, but for what? For not being able to bring her to tears?

I just want to keep walking with her, as if she exists.

Write the part about trying to remove my tear glands, P urges me. Allergies had convinced me, lifting my eyelid to examine, that the little raised dot was an irritant. It can be easy to forget the essential, wearing an old song as if you could hear anything. When you put something on——and wear reversible scenarios, dig oneself out of a borrowed closet and ponder ash. P's voice reverses in memory. Is she sobbing, asking for a referral, longing for the collective? Our tears were for—what were they for?

S was still initiating— meaning, he did not know us well enough to know certain things. He asked off-putting questions, for instance what would we be crying for—beyond the violence we had observed and the news fragments repeating endlessly within our minds and the clutter of our desks or thoughts? He would stop and pass a hand over his brow as if to wipe something away but he looked exactly the same. He was on board with the experiment of chemical signaling as a way to stem violence but when we asked him to cry he needed prolific reasons. This began an onslaught of collective naming, a montage of statements and symbols we began to collect and read aloud when we wished anyone would cry upon command. This assemblage differed from the initial prompts I had composed in that it was culled collectively. It was perhaps the best performative aspect of our plan and made us remember that some of us wanted to write novels or philosophy and yet we didn't think that meant to sit alone in a room thinking. We had no problem with thinking alone in rooms but we were rarely alone and we much preferred anywhere else to a room. We placed a box in the public square labeled, "Reasons to Cry." From these received utterances we began to compile an archive of statements.

P put on her yellow dress, the color of flames, which statistically thus far made more people cry when she read from the list. Studies show that babies cry more in bright yellow rooms. She was merciless. People were activated and their metabolisms rose before she cried. To reproduce the entire list would be tedious but here is a sampling:

Reasons to Cry (from a collective archive)

She was reduced to hiding under a box. Small, empty furniture. That neighborhood is finished. Tears remove toxins, arrow and quiver. I'll never see you again. Ceiling tiles are removed so that rain can cascade from the rotting roof into large trash cans underneath. A seven-year-old boy was laid to rest. Are you sick of yourself? An earthquake. The new cat is getting all of the attention. Coffin, sarcophagus, cemetery monument. This tragedy could have been prevented. Starting with the most basic function of tears, they enable us to see. She really loved him. 500,000 cases of rape are recorded each year in Cameroon. An archway girded with flowers. 200 Methodist clergy in Illinois defy church on same-sex unions. Ripped clothing. You want to believe and have faith that justice works. Pall, pick, spade, pitcher. Military children left behind. A boy in a lonesome autumn day decided to explore the anatomy of a rabbit. Rod or staff. Americanization tastes great. Crash victim remembered. Kitten shot with air rifle in East Ewell. Ship, sickle, skull, skeleton. Remembering the father who perished in Auschwitz. Vessel with flame. Inconsistent weather. Winged face. A bed that has not had my son to lay his head upon. Weeping at tomb. Nobody did anything. Flood evacuees. The willow tree and the urn. She is just so suppressed and frivolous. What I tell my granddaughter about her mother's suicide. Resentments gather in the limbic system. Gentrification. She's not comfortable with human contact. Victims are forced into silence. Cable provider cancelled Lifetime TV. An anchor disguised as a cross. A germaphobic dreams in her sleep. He has to return his MacBook Pro. Slept through the holidays. Dementia patients everywhere. Sacred will I keep thy dear remains.

We were going through a time in which we weren't ourselves and we wondered what it meant to be ourselves without lying or imposing. There never was time to find out who we were. This was easy to admit with eyes closed, late at night, pressed against circumstances which made us fluidly exchange ourselves for other fleeting notions of self. Even if posed, we saw fairly clearly that we weren't anyone. We didn't see ourselves as interchangeable or expendable, yet we knew that we were. We wanted to apply these ideas to making art and living in community. Systematically, we learned that we did not know how to do anything. P lamented that for every book she had considered writing she must learn to unwrite what she had already written. She called it rewiring. I knew that I needed to write and speak more slowly and stop doing what I thought I knew how to do already. We discovered that to do what one knows how to do isn't anything unless it is done as an offering. To create something new, we had to do what we didn't know and that included, especially for O, teaching in a manner in which to demonstrate what he did not know and what he proposed to do about this lack. O said we should experiment and fail and therefore learn. This is not what anyone says aloud. Mostly we want to look smart, especially in certain public roles, but we decided jointly that we must unwrite everything we have written or unspeak every word we have said as a place to begin. No time to fall behind in the project of consciousness. P looked at me adamantly one day and proclaimed that this must be why she can never finish anything, because how does one hold interest in the work of someone who used to be someone else and who all along was lying through every letter?

Can I help it, she asked, if my assumed past means very little? And never mind that none of it, any of what she'd written, was autobiographical in the first place—the fact that it somehow emanated from her made it problematic. We thought that we might attempt the experiment suggested by the brilliant Bernadette Mayer, to get someone else to write for us, pretending to be us, but in this endeavor we failed as well, as we could find no one interested in pretending to be us, except ourselves, and we were already constantly pretending to be each other. We could see the outlines of our individual forms but we did not believe in material separation of our bodies. We imagined that the particular act of finding others to write as us was meant for persons who existed primarily or perhaps too often within their own skin. We considered pretending to be ourselves but this proved too difficult. We considered pretending to write as if we knew something but then decided that that was what we had been doing all along. What we needed to do was to write, speak and live as if we knew nothing. If we could do this then we might find ourselves on our way on the walk of speculatively and positively re-imagining the future.

Our every effort seemed gargantuan. We had to resist getting up to rinse a tea cup, replace a phone in its charger, or scroll through online distractions. We had to resist so many things in order to be still and retrain our minds on the project of reminding ourselves that we knew nothing of ourselves and therefore nothing of our surroundings. AG and H spoke about reorienting ourselves toward empathy as a first effort for our collective. We knew that this was merely a moment of humbling momentum. What of all the other moments, we wondered. We hoped they might begin to coincide and behave less erratically, as we ourselves should.

All of us seemed to share this problem of manifestation, or as HG would say, we wondered how to execute our plans. We wondered how to rise outside the confines of a day to complete tasks other than those set before us through the obligatory nature of bodies within days. It was obvious to us that many humans had propelled themselves beyond minutia which, though not at all compelling, can revise our boundaries until we find that we dwell within trodden basement mire. We are bending over, untangling our perceptions akin to streets, stumbling, dropping and arranging insignificant materials or immaterial concerns. We forget to notice that a bird is lingering by our ear, possibly with a message.

We suffered from a periodic inability to awaken. Sometimes we sat late at night in discussion and when one of us began to doze off we'd get up and slap each other on the cheek, not with any malice or delight, just bracingly. I once witnessed HG squeezing his cheeks between forefinger and thumb, H literally pressing hard upon her navel with a finger as she lay upon her back, P drinking cup after cup of tea, myself walking endlessly to calm my mind until I was barely a smudge upon the sidewalk and O traveling to higher and higher elevations, trying to gain perspective.

I went to see AG in a flight from my endless attempts to wake. He told me that every person could manifest outside the confines of any day, that every moment can unfold until it becomes a universe, vast. I paused for a long time taking this in, so I lost many universes as I strained to open his statement. Could each moment be compelled to behave, to arrange itself in a line within a series of other similarly competent moments? In my imaginings, I assumed that the inherent potential existed in the moment, not in oneself. But AG quickly dispensed with my mirage, as if he had divined my thoughts, saying that every person could attain this unfolding at any time. I was not able to look at him or maybe I could only look but could not hear anything he had to say. I feared the moment might be behaving badly and opening a world of universes I would be compelled to dismiss. But when I could finally bring myself to look I saw that the brightness was not of AG but somehow traveling through him, as a train or a streak of light, and that he made no attempt to hold it, to hold anything, not my attention, not my gaze, not my belief. He was simply inside possibility in a way which was problematically revelatory, because in his presence I could not help but to know certain things. I wondered how H could bear his constant company and then I tried to stop my mind meandering and he told me that we should never abbreviate attempts to rouse, because our realm in each moment is intimate. This statement seemed to undo all of the others I had been describing to myself—moments lined up, behaving themselves, unleashing flashes of light, a recognition—none of it was personal but as this particular moment uncloaked itself I could see a difference between manifestation and *manifestation*. Also a key difference between personal and *personal*. P says I'm being oblique but I'm merely exploring multiple dimensions within these concepts, which aren't necessarily as I formerly supposed them to be. Nor am I, nor must any of us be, and that notion is one tiny hook upon which to rest the cloak as it falls from the moment and we bid ourselves further along.

We thought that we might be anyone, but not "someone" as if someone meant a predetermined we. When we turned around we were still our unknown selves. Where we all began, in what felt like a blight, we were finished and also not yet begun. Our causes were cursive, and bled. What was missing was our sense of how to exist within time and magnetism. What was it that drew us away from our actual natures or causes and into other ridiculous thoughts and acts? We decided that we had not spent enough time contemplating the letters in the palms of our hands, that these letters or drawings were never busy. Our hands were busy and so turned face down so we didn't actually ever see our own actions mirrored in our palms or circumstances. H did not forget to turn hers up to the light. She could read palms, faces, fractions of our expressions and movements. She could read the way the light fell upon our features. She could hold in her gaze something immaterially bright. We appeared to others untouched and we marveled at the invisible nature of our malady. We grasped an elusive 'someone' despite our wish to be anyone, and to be so in unison.

P told me the reason we longed to be *anyone* but fell into possible *someones* was that our chronology was wrong. She claimed that if we simply waited to be anyone, nothing could happen. She claimed that what we must do is to imagine ourselves as adequate *anyones*; then we must think through our causes and write ourselves into existence. This is how we must unlisten and unspeak and strike out anything before that was tentative or doubtful. We must write our causal existence into being where we can first see everything in tangible letters. We must see our tearful enactment exactly and commit it to text.

We turned over our palms now and examined them. We paced the room. We had been waiting as if we could become anyone through the passage of time. What we needed was causal action. Waiting to write an event until after it occurs is missing the opportunity to create an event in thought and language.

I argued that the passage of time is a myth. P scoffed as if that were self-evident. But then she said, "quite," with ironic emphasis, as if admitting that in this way she must revoke her initial prejudice. My voicing the words was a response to her plea to shun inactivity and use language to begin the process of magnetizing actions to words.

I replied, *I'm nobody, who are you?*

And she answered, *How dreary to be somebody.* We laughed because we took refuge in the refrain as if we might finally have not merely admired the words, but conceived an enactment of them.

P did not believe it until I held her wrist and gazed at her palm, dizzyingly, and she into mine. The least plausible outcomes of our narrative became the only viable course of action and none of us cared at all about doubt or failure—which were the volition of *somebodies* who carried about articles of expectation. We tried to carry on as if we had none, only motion and thought and speech acts coupled with written and bodily acts.

Let our archives show, she stated, again up and pacing anew, that we, actively *nobodies* have begun to rewrite our old and stalking selves. Instead of following something uncatchable we were now catching on to our own volition. If we each sought another's permissive garment, or sleeve, we would all be accounted for.

We must *use* ourselves she incanted, adamantly green, and I had to suppress my desire to collect her tears then and there. She saw me mentally reach for a phial, though I had not stirred, and said, *no, they'll only spoil before we get anywhere,* and reassured me as to her endless supply.

What makes me anxious is, I've learned how to close the window properly, finally, and this interior now approaches the inside of P's head. She talks about drowning in our collection of tears. I tell her that is why she feels sick. When I ask her what she wants she says, I want to stand near you and hear you say something. I want to give birth to you. What P wants is something that takes her out of herself, which is not work or consumerism. We begin to see that relationships which once moved a certain way might possibly move in another. And our friends are. Diagrams. Insistence and. Reverie.

I can't help wanting to collect you. Your undergarments. Your movements. Your speech—was what so many men had said to P—or that was how they behaved, as if they might disappear within one small gesture of her hand and suddenly know something necessary to their existence. She had that effect on everyone except herself and to me she was always the memory of that, meaning she created obsessive possibility. I didn't have to be myself if I didn't want to, but mostly I resisted the impulse to abandon.

The only way to be safe was to watch from a miniscule distance. How I saw the moving portrait also changed, and both of us were out of our element in a way we could not admit to anyone else. We relied on each other for a type of anonymity and consolation which became an invisible, contractible shared skin. A sack of malleable milk in which we divined. Quivered. And neither of us moved without import to the other. I was her unwritten book. She could watch me inhabit her text. We thought about making a body constructed of film, a projection that could move and speak, made up of transparent vibrations, filaments and sounds. But our ideas always surpassed our capability. We blamed this on the time of conceptualisms, and though it shouldn't have been believed, it became an excuse for our affectionate and irritating failures.

I dropped out of that book when it became too legible, she said, although her saying she had dropped out was still an admission of involvement. She could deny her entanglement but it was obvious. How could she not be somehow in relation to something abandoned? As if putting deliberate distance between ourselves and something else does anything beyond binding us to distance. So you bend to retrieve something non-material. And danger reassures each wish fragment, fomenting and needing to be stirred, concocted. Another mistake would be to consider her book still as an object, alive upon a desktop, with whorls upon its fingertips and thoughts of mobility. As if becoming an object were necessary for validity.

I took a turn about the room, taking her arm, at first silently, and then in laughter, because it had become crystalline, the book had been paced, it had been torn, it had been stolen, it had been heard and enacted in tears. If that were not enough for some it would be enough for others. The flesh of the book was on her arms. And it was beckoning. She could transpose thought to paper, type and binding, but she could also contain everything.

Acknowledgements

The author is grateful to the following publications, editors, readers and supporters of this project: *Bone Bouquet, Brooklyn Rail, Drunken Boat, Evening Will Come, Event, Jerry, Letterbox, Peaches and Bats, Poets.org, Puerto del Sol, Tarpaulin Sky* and *Zen Monster.* Thanks to Scott Bentley, Anselm Berrigan, Julie Carr, Nikkita Cohoon, Gillian Gerome, Renee Gladman, Leora Fridman, Krystal Languell, Sam Lohmann, Denise Newman, Daniel Saldaña Paris, Christian Peet, Kristin Prevallet, Carmen Gimenez Smith, Joshua Marie Wilkinson and Maged Zaher. Thank you Molly Sutton Kiefer for making this book possible and Noah Saterstrom for continual collaboration and inspiration. Endless thanks to Brad Davidson.

Laynie Browne is a poet, prose writer, teacher and editor. Her most recent collections of poems include *You Envelop Me* (Omnidawn), *P R A C T I C E* (SplitLevel 2015), and *Scorpyn Odes* (Kore Press 2015) Her honors include a 2014 Pew Fellowship, the National Poetry Series Award (2007) for her collection *The Scented Fox*, and the Contemporary Poetry Series Award (2005) for her collection *Drawing of a Swan Before Memory*. Her poetry has been translated into French, Spanish, Chinese and Catalan. She is co-editor of *I'll Drown My Book: Conceptual Writing by Women* (Les Figues Press, 2012) and is currently editing an anthology of original essays on the Poet's Novel. She teaches at University of Pennsylvania and at Swarthmore College.